MERCY MERCY

kelby losack

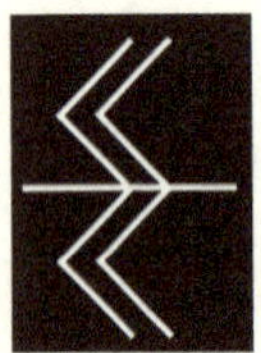

A Broken River Books Original
BROKEN RIVER BOOKS
Oklahoma City, OK

Cover art and interior layout by Kelby Losack
www.kelbylosack.com
Back page art of pyre and wolf woman by Christopher Olson

ISBN: 979-8368048512

Printed in the USA.

Contents

for Dad, for Rowan, and for Phoenix

Abraham took the wood for the burnt offering and placed it on his son Isaac, and he himself carried the fire and the knife. As the two of them went on together, Isaac spoke up and said to his father Abraham, "Father?"

"Yes, my son?" Abraham replied.

"The fire and wood are here," Isaac said, "but where is the lamb for the burnt offering?"

Abraham answered, "God himself will provide the lamb for the burnt offering, my son." And the two of them went on together.

—Genesis 22:6-8

I

S ANCTUARY HAD BEEN A cineplex hundreds of years back, before the moon split. The marquee was busted neon tubes of crooked letters. A crucifix wearing the skull of a deer hung by cables above the entrance. Inside, the priest rehearsed his next sermon to rows of empty theater seats, some of which had been reupholstered with coyote fur. From the entrance where the man who'd been summoned now stood waiting, daylight spilled over the cracked concrete in the shape of a coffin. Constellations of dust motes danced across the man's outstretched shadow.

The priest's lips moved a few beats behind the scripture buzzing distorted from the box implanted in his neck. He quoted:

"Whoever is baptized in the blood will be saved, and whoever is not baptized will be condemned. And these signs will accompany those who believe..."

The latency in his cheaply rigged voice mod caused a delay of several seconds between each sentence, but the priest soldiered on:

"...they will drive out demons... they will speak in new tongues... they will touch fire and not be burned... they will drink poison and not be sick..."

The man rocked on his heels. Hands digging through pockets in search of nothing but an excuse to fidget. The priest prayed:

"Bless us, O Keeper of the Wooded Wasteland, that we may heal the earth... Curse

our bodies to reject circuitry unnecessary for fulfilling your will... and baptize us in blood. Amen."

The priest winced upon ejecting the micro disc from his voice box. Flesh around the implant: black with infection. The man made his way to the stage and took the micro disc from the priest. Tucked it in the fold of his sock.

"Been a while since you've recited from gospel," the man said.

The priest lit up. "So you listen?"

The man shrugged. "Not always in the mood for music. Sermons are the perfect length for a drive to the city. I'll get this chopped down and bring it back tonight."

The man turned to leave. The priest hopped down from the stage and followed.

Voice box glitching into a munk-high pitch: "That wasn't all I called you for."

The man stopped.

The priest smacked the mod on his neck. In a sludge-thick baritone, he said, "Meet me in my office?"

The man nodded. Followed the priest up a dark staircase to the projection booth. A dingy cubicle decorated in tattered posters. Metal tables littered with antiquated tech, gutted in a mess of circuitry, plastic, and screws. The priest's second calling was rigging relics of the old world to give them new functionality. And whenever his tinkering seemed in vain, scraps could be sold down in the city. Cameras especially were favorable junk to back-alley surgeons in the underground optic game. Much as the priest demonized luxury mods as sins against the flesh, he knew people were people, and as long as there were chrome heads plucking out their organic eyes in exchange for rigs with HUD and infrared and god only knows what other capabilities, the church may as well get a cut.

The priest flipped on the holoprojector and a golden glow filled the cramped booth. On the stage below were indiscernible holographic flickerings from a scratched-up disc. The projector was strictly for ambiance.

The priest crossed his arms over the back of a foldout chair. The man leaned against the wall.

"The keeper's slumber is near its end," the priest said. "This season's offerings have been chosen."

The rest of their conversation would echo in the man's head on his slow walk through the village to meet the boy, accompanied by the looped memory of his son's birth: the tub full of bloody water; his sweat-drenched wife reaching up to hug his neck, to cry against his cheek; the powerful, shrill screams of their baby boy.

The man said, "I haven't been a member of the church since-"

He let the sentence hang there.

"You are a part of the community," the priest said. "You are a part of the church."

Over the spinning gears and clanking metal spilling out from the bullet barn, the echoes continued.

"I'm not protesting for myself," the man said, "but I'm barely twice the boy's age. The ritual is one old and one young, yeah?"

"What matters," the priest said, the lag in his distorted words only amplifying the man's anxiety, "is the condition of the soul. And yours is quite worn. This election is a symbol of mercy."

Over the tranquil tune hummed by a mid-shift gardener, the man said, "What about the well? Hasn't the boy been crucial to the digging project?"

Over the bubbling/sizzling/cackling from the diner, the priest said, "You are both of utmost importance to this community."

The man stopped at the fur post. And the priest's words echoed: "That's what makes it a sacrifice."

II

T HE FUR TRAPPER SNAPPED her
fingers in the man's face. Brought
him back to present.

"You buying or admiring?" she said.
"Either will cost you."

The trapper was young. Could tell by
her stature and the brightness of her
eyes, but especially by the runes carved in
her cheeks. Only the young bloods were
doing that shit, the kids even younger
than the man's son. She had no idea who
he was, or the legacy of the role she'd
been assigned, and it made the man feel
ancient.

Hanging on the trapper's wall amongst satchels and blankets was a coat, thick and golden with blood red tips. The man said, "What kind of beast did that come from?"

"Some nameless cat," the trapper said. "Vicious creature, but beautiful. Didn't want to do it to her. I was chasing a rabbit when she came out of nowhere, her mind made up which way it'd go down. If I'd have kept it peaceful, I wouldn't be here."

"How much?"

The trapper rubbed the black horns of her headdress. Jagged symbols carved all up and down her arms. "Rarity alone puts a high tag on it. Plus, I just told you how dangerous it was to acquire. Not to mention the time spent sewing."

The man checked his bracelet. "I'll give you two thousand."

"Say fucking less."

The man dialed in the amount and squeezed his wrist to send the funds and the trapper checked her bracelet. Buffering lines blinking slowly. She held her wrist out closer to his. The lines continued to blink. She untangled a cord from her satchel and the funds went through soon as she plugged in. Then she unplugged their wrists from each other and tossed him the coat and the man pressed his face into the fur, eyes closed, and he stood like that for an uncomfortably long time before telling her thank you and continuing on his way to meet up with the boy he'd been chosen to die with.

III

THE BOY TIGHTENED THE screws in his left elbow a half-turn at a time, stretching his arm to full length and then flexing to check the resistance. When it felt right to him again, he pocketed the screwdriver and tipped the spout of a tin can between his fingers, oil washing over the pistons in his hand and the hydraulics in his forearm.

It was the spiky-haired kid's turn on the well digger, a big-ass drill the shape of a spinning top. He was having a time of it. Vibrations rippling from his death grip on the handlebars all the way up into his skull. Feet planted on either side of a widening hole as he leaned his weight into the machine and held steady pressure on the trigger, trying not to get torqued up in a bind and launched spiraling into the air with one of his arms still caught up in the free-spinning beast below, blood spraying from the severed socket.

He'd seen it happen before.

The boy finished doctoring his junk-rigged appendage and dug a different set of tools from his jacket pockets: a cylindrical mess of copper tubing and coils and a balloon full of what looked like shards of orange glass. He pinched the kaza with his organic fingers so as not to risk dropping any of it and sprinkled a dose of the crystallized chemical dregs down the chute of the lung torch. He held the torch between skeletal iron fingers and hit that shit. Felt the knives slide down his throat and his chest catch fire and a few seconds later, he felt amazing. The world was suddenly brighter, more colorful. A flood of endorphins washed away all the pain in his body and he was ready to fucking GOOOO, at least for a good minute or two, until his heart rate settled and his vision dulled to normal and he was back to coasting. Numb. His preferred state of being.

The well digger hacked up black clouds and shot clumps of dirt at the spiky-haired kid's face. Even over the gasoline smell, he caught a whiff of the kaza—that unmistakable blend of berries and cat piss. He hollered at the boy, "Don't be greedy!"

The boy pocketed the lung torch. "Gotta stretch it out," he said. "Dad ain't re-upped yet."

The spiky-haired kid eased off the machine's trigger and grit his teeth as it rattled to a stop. "Here," he said. "Since you're all good and high now." He backed away from the hole, now hip-deep to most but more like chest-deep to the two of them. He massaged his wrists.

The boy said, "Lemme show you how a real one does it," but before he could crank the starter, his dad came up on them wearing a crazy fur coat.

The boy said, "When'd you get back?"

"Just now," the man said. He nodded at the boy's new arm. "How's it feel?"

"Hurts all the way up in my jaw most the time. But I'm not spazzing out as much."

The man said, "That's good." He didn't know how to invite his son to die in the name of keeping a violent god satiated and willing to grant blessings another year. Didn't think the boy would go for it anyway. Each generation seemed less and less faithful. So he said, "I was thinking we'd set out on a hunt tomorrow."

"What about the well?"

"I'm sure the one you dug up on the east side won't dry up overnight."

The boy smiled. Something the man hadn't seen in a long time.

"I have a run to make," the man said, "but I'll be back tonight."

The boy said, "And we'll go hunting."

And the man said, "Yeah. We'll go hunting."

IV

A SKINNED DEER CARCASS flew across the black sky then plummeted through a blur of seizure-inducing holo-ads and every color neon, the city street rushing up to meet it with a wet kiss. The carcass erupted, splattering gore all over the windshield of the first car too late to hit the brakes. Chunks of it bounced from bumper to bumper and got chewed up under a dune runner on its way back in from the desert. A leg flew off and smacked against the door of a steel body pickup riding on mud tires.

The rookie behind the wheel tensed up. Said, "The fuck?"

The man riding shotgun said, "That happens sometimes. Flip a bitch at this next light and take the ramp."

The rookie did as the man said, eyes darting everywhere as the man gave directions.

Every inch of concrete in the city was tattooed in some kind of graffiti, whether neon or paint. Along the walls beneath an overpass: colorful words bent into illegible sigils/a muscled-up buck really giving it to a big-tittied stick figure from behind/the words PUSSY ASS BOAAAA floating from the snout of a howling wolf. Look up and you'd see a web of cables strung between brutalist concrete structures that stacked up to the clouds. Shopping centers on top of Head Trip lounges on top of apartment complexes on top of pharmacies boasting thirty-second prescriptions. You could tell the majority class of each district by the level of mod heads braving the sidewalk. Wealthy bitches with so much work done you could see the hardware glowing between the cracks in their flesh-painted chrome shells. You'd spot low lifes booted up with just as many mods, only sporting more scars.

The man's guidance had them detour through medical, market, and art districts to help ease the rookie into it. Kid was a born church member with a happy home life and love of nature. Couldn't just toss him in the deep end. Even the better sites of the city seemed to have brought him to the border of awestruck wonder and catatonic shock.

Clouds of steam billowed out from grab-and-go ramen and taco huts. The man cracked his window. Smells of ginger and chili powder wafted into the cab. The rookie breathed it in and relaxed a bit.

The man was finally done playing tour guide. He told the rookie where to turn and they passed through a tunnel lined with tents and barrel fires and came out the other side into the slums. More or less it was just like anywhere else in the city, except the people on the corners weren't waiting for a crossing signal. Alleyways functioned as living room furniture displays. Vending machines spat out sex toys and corporatized drugs.

The man said, "Pull up here," pointing to a parking space beneath the fluorescent green glow of an eyeball centered inside an open palm.

The rookie parked at the end of a row of motorcycles and the man told him how it would go down.

You'd go in through the psychic's entrance and up a stairwell behind a beaded curtain. Knock on the door at the top of the stairs and smile for the camera.

"Is there a password?"

"What? No, there's a camera."

Once inside, you'd be patted down by the plug. Weapons were fine—you'd be made for a mark without at least a pistol or a razor on you—but the plug's hands were geared up with x-ray mods wired into his optics, and if his palms read a mic implant or merc bomb, he'd flatline you on sight.

Three reasons there'd be no bodyguards:

1. The plug trusted nobody.

2. There were turrets in at least one corner of every room that the plug could control with his mind.

3. The plug was fast as fuck with a katana.

The rookie said, "I have questions."

The man sighed. "I can't think of a single thing I left out, but go ahead."

"I'm replacing you as the delivery driver, right?"

The man nodded.

"So... can't I just load up my bracelet with the dues and take a list into the city, pick up the goods in that brightly lit shopping district?"

The man looked at the rookie like he had two heads. "Yeah," he said. "That's pretty much the best way to do it."

"Then why are we here? This guy sounds like a drug dealer or something."

"Oh, right, right, right." The man reached into his sock and pulled out the micro disc from the priest's voice box. "The priest likes to record his sermons beforehand to get all the lag and distortion smoothed out. The plug is a wizard editor. He'll get it chopped down and equalized in seconds."

"Fantastic, so we'll just be in and out."

"You will be, yeah." The man opened his door and got out. Said, "But he's also my drug dealer."

The rookie followed the man inside the psychic's entrance. Nodded hello to the rune-scarred receptionist. Then it was up the stairs for the pat-down, just like the man had explained.

The plug said, "Green to go." Shouldered a sheathed katana like a baseball bat. He wore jersey shorts and bunny house slippers and ten gold chains draped over a heavily tattooed torso. He dabbed the man up and said, "I dig the fur."

The man introduced the rookie.

The plug flashed a chrome smile and said, "Come on in. Pop a squat."

The three of them dropped down on a horseshoe couch. Holovid rig set up in the center playing a classic samurai joint. The man passed the disc between the holographic sword fight on display and the disc disappeared inside a slot in the plug's neck. His pupils lit up in rapidly flashing soundwaves. "When you getting net connection up in the hills, man? This type of shit could be handled over email."

"Major focus right now is on water," the man said. "Priorities."

"Nah, I feel that." The plug reached under the couch and pulled out a large vase-like chem rig.

Rookie caught the vibe shift. "I'm going to go wait in the truck," he said. And to the plug: "It was nice to meet you."

"For sure," the plug said, dipping into a plastic bag fat with shards of kaza, sprinkling a healthy pinch into the glass bowl of the rig. When the rookie left, he said, "New guy's strictly business, huh?"

"He'll break eventually," the man said.

The plug ejected the disc from his neck and handed it back. Said, "Done." He torched the bowl and took a deep rip off the kaza bong and coughed. Passed the rig and lighter across to the man, who mimicked the ritual. Without asking, the plug retrieved an ounce of the shit from a lock box in his bedroom. Dropped the chems on the console in front of the man and the man stuffed the shit in his jacket pocket. Dialed up 1k on his bracelet for the kaza and another hundo for the chopped audio. It went through immediately.

The plug said, "Preciate you."

The man said, "Always," and he got up to leave, but the plug stopped him.

"Hold up," he said. "I got my hands on some shit I ain't supposed to show nobody. But it's too cool not to show nobody."

The man said, "You know I'm nobody."

The plug pointed his katana at the man. Said, "That's why I'ma show you."

The plug went to his lock box again and came back with a candy-painted green cell blaster. The gun was four and a half feet long from the butt to the hexagonal barrel, wide enough to slide your arm inside. "Two-point-five second charge rate," the plug said. "This baby's rigged with modified ammo. Secret military shit. Supposed to launch a projectile that expands by 500% on impact before exploding. Nicknamed the god killer. Designed to kill gods."

The man said, "How'd you get that?"

"That's a long-ass story with a longer list of self-incriminating details I ain't willing to divulge." He climbed over the back of the couch, laid the giant gun across his lap. "Bitch of it is, now I got it, who I'm supposed to sell this shit to? I don't fuck with the psychos. And if I scrap it for parts, no street rat will appreciate or understand the components enough to pay what it's worth. I don't even know what the fuck it's made of besides reputation. So I guess what you looking at, Mr. Nobody, is my most dangerous trophy."

A kneeling samurai on the holovid opened his robe and disemboweled himself with a tanto blade. Holographic guts spilled over the clutter of flash drives, magazines, and chem shards on the console.

The man said, "How much?"

The plug smiled. "Heh, you funny."

"How much?"

"Your life, nigga."

"Okay, I'll take it."

"Fuck would you even do with this kind of artillery?"

"Haven't made up my mind yet," the man said. "It's a plan B."

Another swordsman stepped up behind the gutless samurai and raised his sword skyward. "If you on some ecoterrorist type shit," the plug said, the samurai's head sliced clean off his shoulders, "you can miss me with that. That's all you and the other hillbillies. You feel me?"

The man said, "It's much more personal than that."

"They make blades and pistols for personal shit."

The man said nothing.

The plug thought it over. A battlefield scene filled the space between them. Arrows flying from horseback archers. Cannon balls decapitating men mid-war cry. "My surgeon's got kind of a side gig she always tryna pull me into," the plug said. "Organ harvesting shit. Ain't been desperate enough to go down that road, you feel me? Chems and weapons turn to green before I've barely touched them. I know you ain't got the green for it, but you are still an organic nigga, right?"

The man said, "Through and through."

"How bad you want this? 'Cause what I'ma propose is an evil-ass bargain if you ain't really bout it."

"I'ma disappear after tonight either way. You're bargaining with a ghost."

"Ghost ain't got a need for a heart then, right?"

"You'd be doing me a favor ripping that out."

"I ain't ripping shit. But if we have a deal, let's go see the surgeon."

The man shrugged behind the screaming bloody face of a translucent samurai. Said, "Then let's go see the surgeon."

V

HE BOY KICKED HIS muddy boots off at the door. Sunset cutting in red, white, and blue through the stars and stripes draped over the glass. The flag was a relic from the old world, from when his folks would scavenge shit from the ghost towns in the woods. Other relics decorated the single-wide: amber bottles of perfume, gemstones of all shapes and colors, and–hanging high on the kitchen wall where a clock might once have gone–a chrome rim with spokes protruding eighteen inches to a wing-tipped center, the wheels of an ancient street war chariot. The boy's mom had arranged these artifacts in a certain way to contrast and compliment the interior of the trailer, itself a refurbished relic with faded floral wallpaper and checkered linoleum floors. Not a thing had been moved or even touched since it'd last been placed by her hand. Maybe blanketed in dust or buried under empty beer cans, but other than that, the arranging of artifacts froze where she'd left them, an attempt to keep some essence of her tethered to the home.

"He made it back yet?" the girl said.

The boy shook his head.

The girl followed him inside.

Straight to the bedroom: a scattering of clothes on the floor/lucky cat waving from a bedside table/posters of chromed-out clowns wielding hatchets, their necks adorned with icy chains. Whole room glowed a rippling blue from the hololamp his dad had brought back from the city.

They sat at the edge of the bed and the boy kissed the girl gently and she bit his lip and slid a hand over his crotch. He jabbed his tongue in her mouth and they peeled each other's clothes off and she shoved him to his back and straddled him. Melting as she slid over his cock and bent forward to nibble his ear, to kiss the thick pink scar tissue encircling the plate that held his iron arm in socket. Fingers interlaced, she brought his organic hand to her breast and his iron hand to her throat and the boy squeezed both as she rode him. Hips bucking hard against each other. The girl moaned and panted. The boy bit his lip, trying not to bust too quick. He felt the walls of her pussy tighten and she trembled. Got hers. She pulled his hand away from her throat and slipped off his cock and spun around, slid her dripping pussy up his stomach, over his chest. Thrust the air above his lips.

He worked his tongue in circles over her clit and she licked the tip of his cock before swallowing it, working it up and down with her mouth, tongue going crazy snaking around his shaft. The girl shivered at the coldness of the boy's iron hand on her left butt cheek. He lapped at her folds and flicked her clit with the tip of his tongue. Thirsty for it. She got hers off again and then he busted in her mouth and she swallowed and collapsed on top of him and when she caught her breath, she curled up against him under a heavy bear fur throw, his blanket since he could just barely walk and talk, could just barely articulate that it was the bear that he wanted from the display at his mom's fur post, and so it was the bear that he got, and no one in the village had shit to say about it.

The boy kissed the girl on the top of her head and dug the lung torch from his jacket hanging off the bed. He hit the kaza and blew smoke at the ceiling and passed the torch to the girl and she did the same.

For a while they just lay there, fingers tracing each other's scars and dimples.

Then the girl said, "I heard there are places in the city you go just to dance. People pack into cramped rooms with different colored lights flashing all over the place and music so loud it rattles your teeth and you can dance all night long."

The boy said, "We'll dance every night when we get there."

"Are you going to tell him?"

"Yeah."

"Promise?"

"Yeah. I promise."

The girl kissed the boy's neck. Said, "We'll stroll through botanical gardens. We'll take trips out to the desert and watch all the colors strobe and glow above the cityscape. We'll go to museums to learn about the old world and we'll try all kinds of food and we'll ride the hovertrain everywhere until we can afford a motorcycle."

"And we'll have sex," the boy said.

"Lots of it."

"Hell yeah. The city is going to be great."

VI

ORGANIC HEARTS WENT FOR up to 500k, so the deal was simple: the man would get his torn out and replaced with a mech pump of questionable performance in exchange for the god killer. The plug would have to bargain his cut with the surgeon, but any way they split it, it'd be more green on the bracelet than the plug had seen in a minute.

Now, a lot of city folk go chrome to some extent, but most will layer flesh-colored shells on top of all the hardware. You can still see the glow and the gears through cracks in their plastic skin, but at a distance and out of touch, they maintain the familiarity of the organic human form.

Every society's got its freaks, though.

The surgeon was this chromed-out freaky bitch, head to shoulders reflecting the jittery fluorescents that lit up a sub-level operating garage. She'd given herself a candy-coated paint job, every uncovered bit of her a glossy turquoise, with emerald orbs where her eyeballs used to be and purple synthetic hair in a pixie cut. Arms decorated in random flash art: a three-eyed tiger/Santa Muerte/kawaii pin-up girls.

But the impressive shit was what you couldn't see. The surgeon was modded the fuck out from synaptic signal boosters coating her skeletal frame to oculars loaded up with x-ray, neural, and thermal analysis software, none of which was needed to read the rookie the second he shuffled in behind the man and the plug.

"If you're gonna watch," she told him, "you're cleaning up your own vomit."

And so the rookie bowed out and chose once again to wait out in the truck, this time wishing for tinted windows and pretending not to notice the hobo orgy spilling out from a tent further up the alley. Flickering orange glow of a barrel fire cast a chain of shadows all knotted together and thrusting up the walls.

The rookie heard one of the hobos break down in a hollering fit. Watched him in the rearview as he stumbled and slipped on the rain-slick concrete, sparks flying between the fingers of a hand cupped over his left eye.

The rookie turned on the radio. Tuned through the trance and bounce shit and stopped on a gorewave station and cranked it up and shrunk as low as he possibly could into the seat.

Inside the surgeon's basement garage, the man removed the loud fur coat, a moth-eaten sweater, and a stained white tee and draped the pile of clothes over a metal table. He lay back in the leather operating chair and squinted against the triburst lights in his face. The surgeon tightened the cuffs around his wrists and ankles.

Precautions.

Because some patients were squirmers, some were thrashers, and some messes can never be cleaned up.

The surgeon shook up a can of blackout mist and uncapped it and screwed it into the mouth of a plastic mask.

The man said, "Hold up."

The plug rolled from one side of the garage to the other in a spinning chair.

The man said, "What's stopping you from gutting me open and taking everything?"

The plug crashed against a rolling drawer cabinet and sent a handful of tools clattering across the floor. The surgeon arched her synthetic brows. The plug said, "My bad."

To the man, the surgeon said, "If I was gonna gut you and toss you, you'd be knocked out in an ice bath, okay? I'm not a fucking merc. I'm an artist." She held the mask over the man's mouth and nose, fogging up his vision before he could say sorry. "Now," she said, "count backwards from ten."

The man was out cold by seven, and the surgeon got to work.

The man could hear the whirring of a circular saw and the cracking of bones from the abyss in which he floated and when he snapped back, he was spread out across the backseat of the truck. God killer in the floorboard. Everything bounced around the cab as the rookie traversed the rocky roads winding up to the village.

The man tried sitting up. Regretted it. Lay there groaning.

The rookie said, "How do you feel?"

The man said, "Like my chest has been ripped open." He lifted his shirt to check that his chest had been stitched back together and, yeah, it had–no less than thirty stitches making an asymmetrical X over where his heart used to be. "Fucking artist, huh?" he said.

Gravel crunched as the rookie slowed to a stop. Headlights beaming on a stretch of road going off into dark nothing. Trees lining either side of the road, barely visible.

"If I keep doing this," the rookie said, "am I going to end up like you?"

"Ain't the job that made me," the man said. "Ain't the city, either. You wanna hold onto your heart, you do just that. Don't go falling in love. Don't go starting a family."

The man struggled to breathe. He wheezed and pounded his chest. Regretted that, too.

The rookie said, "Surgeon wanted to see you back in twenty-four hours. Three days, max."

The man laughed. Said, "Oh, god, it hurts."

"She said the longest one of those mech pumps has ever lasted is ten days, and that was one of the better models. She said she might could tinker with it, though. Work with you on the right diet and chems. I didn't tell her anything. Figured if you hadn't mentioned not being around no more, why should I bring it up."

"You did right," the man said. "Before he eats me alive, I'll be sure to tell god you're a great driver."

The man slid back into the abyss, and the rookie drove on.

VII

THE MAN AWOKE IN his bed with a new kind of tightness in his chest. Fur coat laid out next to him, tucked in on what used to be her side. He got up and dug the hunting packs from under crushed beer cans and dirty clothes that spilled from the closet. He unzipped the packs and checked the inventory: knives with gut hooks, boxes rattling with .40 caliber and 5.56 cartridges, a med kit, water purifying tablets (which the man tossed into the pile of trash on his floor), ratchet straps, holomap blinking a low battery warning. The man punched in coordinates of the mountaintop altar–numbers burned in his brain from years back–then he tossed the holomap back inside the pack with no intention of pulling it out again.

He grabbed a pair of 5.56 hunting rifles from the clutter of guns leaned up against the wall and tested the action on each of them and tossed them on the bed. Tucked a powder blue .40-cal ghost pistol in his waistband. Trusted the boy would be packing his own, a 3D-printed Chiappa rip-off with a seven-inch barrel, .357 mag, black and yellow because he was mom's little b.

And the god killer...

The man wondered just how big a hole it'd leave, how many memories it'd blow out at once if he put it in his mouth and pulled the trigger. He clenched his eyes shut and pictured the scene as he put his whole face inside the barrel. Pulled away at the sound of footsteps and whispers.

"How many nights has she stayed here?"
he'd ask the boy over eggs and coffee.

And the boy would say, "I ain't been
keeping it a secret. You just ain't around
much." And the room would go to spinning
and the man would drop his fork and take
a sharp breath as the machine in his chest
quivered.

"I didn't mean it no type of way," the boy
would say then, and the man would pound a
fist against his chest and wave off the boy's
concern, blame it on the eggs falling down
the wrong pipe, whole time thinking, Not
yet, not already.

And when the rhythm of his artificial
ticker leveled out, he'd say to the boy, "Let's
go bag a beast."

VIII

WITH THEIR PACKS ON their backs and their rifles slung over their shoulders, they left the village for the woods. Thick cables snaked around tall black trees and draped like vines between branches. The cables hummed with electricity and entangled every tree in the forest. Flowers dubbed widow makers were thankfully out of season, giant purple petals concealing vortexes of razor sharp teeth. The man kept several paces ahead of the boy as they trekked over shifting terrain, not saying a word, the boy keeping to the man like a shadow.

IX

F LOCK OF CROWS FEASTING inside
the ribcage of a blind coyote. Dead
eyes: milky white. Tongue hanging out like
a deflated balloon. Bones picked clean. A
feral rodent ran into the center of the flock
and snatched the end of an intestine and
took off with it. Caws of angry birds at its
back. It dashed inside of its burrow, the
bloody entrails slithering in behind it like
a filleted snake. Insects with pearlescent
thoraxes swarmed the stagnant lunar ponds
that were home to poisonous koi and
three-eyed toads. Every inch of the woods
breathed with life, but anything worth

upping a rifle at resided deeper inside of her.

X

T HE BOY FINALLY BROKE the silence. Rambled on about the radar they'd been using to find springs underground. "It's this janky-ass box with little teeth on the bottom of it that you jab into the dirt," he said, "and it's got a screen that shows these colorful horizontal bars and all the colors–the blues and greens, the yellows and reds–they all got a meaning to them, but I forget. Main thing is that the teeth in the ground send out this electromagnetic pulse and if there's water underground, the pulse will echo back and the bars on the screen will go all wavy. But sometimes you

get a ghost echo, like there was a spring
or river running down there at some point
a long-ass time ago maybe, and the earth
remembers that, and that's how you get
a ghost echo and end up drilling a dozen
holes a hundred feet deep just to keep
coming up dry."

XI

THEY CAME UPON A creek half a dozen bodies wide–an exact measurement as told by the bones of moon drinkers stretched across the bed–and they stopped. Watched the gentle flow moving in both directions far as they could see. Sunlight fractured kaleidoscopic over the water.

"We'll have to cross it," the man said. "How do your boots look?"

The boy picked up his left foot, then his right, showing the leather worn off the steel in the toe areas, the smooth soles, the holes in the ankles. He shrugged.

"It's drinking that's the problem, though, right?"

The man stared through the crystal clear water into the hollow sockets of a moon drinker's skull. Licked his lips. Said, "Just to be safe. Try not to fall in."

The boy leapt from rock to rock behind the man, one foot at a time, arms out for balance.

When they made it across without falling in the lunar poison stream, the man ruffled the boy's hair and told him good job and they walked on.

XII

T HE BOY SAID, "WHAT'S the city like?"

And the man said, "It's filthy, but it's also kind of beautiful. It's like all the ugliness and sin in the world dressed up in glitter and chrome."

"What about the people there?"

"Miserable."

"Is that why you spend so much time there?"

"Mmhmm."

XIII

CARCASSES FLEW ACROSS THE sky-meteors of meat raining down blood. The boy raised his hood. The man wiped his brow. They walked on.

XIV

T HE BOY SAID, "TELL me a story about mom."

XV

THE MAN'S WHOLE DEMEANOR softened. He slowed his pace to walk shoulder-to-shoulder with the boy and he said, "Your mom was a market peddler when we lived in the city. She pushed product for this secondhand dealer who came across used mods and homemade rigs, plus some other little shit. Holovids and knock-off designer purses, that sort of shit. She'd slip some of the product for herself, lowkey. We eventually had a collection of pirated Head Trips. We'd lie in bed and plug in and go to all kinds of places—botanical gardens, glaciers, forests where the trees weren't choked by cables. One of these Head Trips was a beach where the water was so clear, you could swim out and if you looked down, you could see the coral and sand along the bottom and all the jellyfish swimming around you. And those jellyfish... fuck. The feeling inputs on these pirated Trips were unpredictable. Sometimes you'd be seeing shit like it was right there in front of you, only you couldn't feel nothing, not even the air around you—like that floaty out-of-body feeling you get when you're dreaming—and sometimes things felt more than real, like the artificial nerve receptors were tweaked to amp up pain and orgasms and–you know, whatever. But the jellyfish. I knew the beach Head Trip was one of those tweaked ones because the water was so frigid it felt like your bones turned to ice, which felt great. But fuck the jellyfish. Their sting was like shards of glass slipped under your skin while at the same time, you've got your tongue clamped to a car battery. I got stung by at least a million of them bitches."

"What about mom?" the boy said. "She made you feel better?"

"No," the man said, "she swam untouched just an arm's length away and called me a pussy."

The man laughed. Then his face twisted up and he grit his teeth and sniffed. Walked a few paces ahead of the boy.

XVI

THEY WALKED ALONG THE stone wall of a burnt down estate—acres of splintered lumber and broken glass atop mounds of ash. Through a toppled section of the wall, the boy spotted a two-headed deer craning one of its necks to bite at the fruit of a scrawny tree, a stubborn survivor of the estate's orchard. The deer's twin head was on a swivel, watching out for predators, like the unseen boy who propped his rifle up on the wall and admired the creature through the scope.

The man held a knot in his throat. Prayed the boy wouldn't shoot and end the hunt right there, forcing the man to invent another lie to press onward.

But then the boy lowered his rifle and shouldered it. Said, "It's beautiful."

"You're not going to take the shot?" the man said.

Between the twin heads, this buck was carrying a forty-point rack and enough meat on its bones to fill a rented freezer in the city for at least a year.

The boy just shook his head and pressed on, not wanting the hunt to end yet.

XVII

THE MAN PLUCKED A beetle from a tree to show the boy.

"You know what this is?"

"Yeah," the boy said. "It's a bug."

"This is a cochineal beetle. The guts of this little guy is where the color purple comes from." The man held his hand out flat and the beetle wriggled across his palm. He said, "Everything in the world—even color—comes from sacrifice."

The boy held his hand out beneath his father's and the man dropped the beetle into the boy's iron palm. The cochineal beetle wriggled to the tip of his index finger, then over the pins and springs of his knuckles and up the welded plate of his wrist. By the time the cochineal beetle got caught up in the hydraulic tubing where the boy's forearm met his elbow, the boy had forgotten about it. He followed his father deeper into the woods, a trail of purple dripping from his fingertips.

XVIII

DECADES AFTER HALF THE moon fell to earth, a new forest had overtaken remnants of the old world left behind. Grass shot up through crumbled streets. Buildings were choked out by weeds. Trees were topped with engine blocks ripped from the junk cars they grew inside of. The man and the boy made their way through one of these towns, stepping lightly with their rifles drawn. These ghost towns had at times been haven to fugitives and moon-drunk mutants.

In a field of waist-high grass, they stepped through a maze of granite slabs scribed with names and numbers. Rows and rows of crosses.

The boy said, "What is this place?"

The man said, "Folks from the old world used to bury their dead in the ground, and they'd mark the spot where they buried them with decorated stones."

"What for?"

"To remember, I guess."

The boy was quiet for a while. Then he said, "I can't decide if I'd like that or not."

"To be buried?" the man said.

"To always remember."

A low roar, then a rustling in the grass.

The man and the boy upped their rifles and scoped the area.

Didn't catch it before it charged. An albino boar leaking lunar poison from open rotgut rushed at them, thrashing side to side, knocking over crosses. The beast was closing too fast to get a clear sight through the scope, so the man dropped the rifle.

Pulled the pistol from his waistband. The boy froze behind him and didn't blink. The man squeezed the trigger, and the first shot sent him back to the narrow hallway outside the boy's bedroom. The boy is three years old, pounding his little fists against the door his father holds shut from the other side, screaming until he's shaking and gasping for breath and then screaming some more, choking on the tears and snot he's sucking in through trembling lips.

"Daddy, DADDY! NO HURT MOMMY!"

Her eyes gone milky white. Foaming at the mouth and thrashing against the walls. Getting up stronger and angrier each time the man kicked her to the ground, until she finally crawled away and came back charging with a knife.

The man emptied the clip.

The boar's chin smacked the ground so hard it bit its own tongue in half. Skidded to a stop at the man's feet.

The man clenched his jaw and shook all over and walked on before the tears fell.

Fourteen years later, he could still hear the boy's screams. Was all he could hear, even as the boy stood there now, calling out to him.

When the man wouldn't stop or turn, the boy picked up his rifle, choking on the spoiled meat and sewage smell emitting from the hole in the boar's stomach. Then he ran to catch up to his father and threw his arms around him and wouldn't let him go, hard as he fought.

XIX

THE MAN AND THE boy lied to each other at the same time, said they had to piss, and they split off in separate directions.

The man knelt behind a dumpster and prayed. "What am I doing, my love? Which way do I go about this?" He held his face in his hands, smothering the sounds of his own sobbing.

The boy really did have to piss-stood saturating the peeled leather seat of a junker sitting on raw wheels-but he also needed a hit. Checked over his shoulder to be sure his dad wasn't around, then he took out the torch and sucked the kaza deep into his chest. He zipped up and took a stroll down the street, feeling the ghosts that haunted the blown-out laundromat, barbershop, and bakery.

A high-pitched wail from up the road made him choke on another hit. He ducked behind a bench. The shrill wailing grew louder, closer. The boy upped his rifle over the back of the bench and scoped it out. Shuffling bare-ass naked across an intersection was a woman biting into the live rodent she gripped in both hands. The woman's sharp teeth tore into the mangled thing's shoulder and ripped out flesh and tendons and she chewed. Blood spilling over her lips and down her chin, between her breasts, past her navel. Only thing the woman wore was a black wolf headdress. The boy's heart pounded. The wolf woman faced him in the crosshairs and smiled. The boy shouldered his rifle and took off running until his dad called to him, stumbling out of an alley and reeking of kaza himself.

"What's the matter?" the man said.

The boy looked up the street to the intersection, could no longer see the wolf woman or her screaming meal. He caught his breath and shook his head. Said, "Nothing."

XX

S TORM ROLLED IN. THE sky grew dimmer until it faded to black. Lightning danced across the tops of the trees and the thing in the man's chest switched the beat up. The man and the boy pulled their hoods over their heads, stuffed their hands in their pockets as the rain fell. They searched for cover, for a cave or a tree with no cables running through it. No luck with either.

XXI

A BOLT OF LIGHTNING hit a frayed cable draped low between two trees and it gave off a deafening clap and then a second bolt shot from the cable into the man's chest and his feet left the earth for a split second before he fell limp facedown in the mud and the boy gripped his collar in an iron fist and dragged the man through the mud until he found a toppled over tree with roots thick enough to hide beneath and he waited out the storm holding his toasted ragdoll dad in his arms, rocking him, pretending it was the other way around.

XXII

THE RAIN QUIT FALLING and the sun returned behind a translucent haze of grey and the boy carried the man over his shoulders like a bagged deer. High off the dizziness all the baggage brought upon him. Pistol and revolver tucked in his waistband; both of their packs strapped to his back; hunting rifles slung over his right shoulder; god killer in his iron hand. The gun was too loudly colored to make sense as a hunting rifle, too heavy to make sense wanting to lug around the woods with no intention of using it. What the hell was his dad expecting to come up against?

A sound like a rusty spring uncoiling echoed through the woods, in sync with the boy's steps, as if the old and worn earth were creaking beneath his feet. The boy kept to the cover of the trees and watched the corpse thrower toss a skinned deer into the bucket of a catapult and throw the lever, launching the carcass into the air. The meteor of meat flew high above the trees until it shrunk out of sight.

A crow perched on a branch above the boy's head craned its neck. Tiny gears whirred and clicked. The crow opened its beak and the corpse thrower spoke through it.

"I can see you."

The boy said to the crow, "We're just passing through. My dad's hurt."

"What happened to him?"

"Got hit by lightning."

From behind the boy, mumbled through a tightly coiled iron jaw, the corpse thrower said, "Why you still talking to the bird?"

The boy jumped back and aimed from the hip with the god killer.

The corpse thrower showed his palms, said, "How bout we stay peaceful? I've buried bombs–just saying, not threatening–but I've buried bombs all over these woods, and they're all synced up with this." The corpse thrower unbuttoned his shirt to show what looked like a cast iron spider with wires and tubes for legs piercing into his heart. "I flatline," he said, "and it's like the rest of the moon dropped to earth."

"What's the purpose of that?" the boy said.

The corpse thrower towered over the boy, his body a patchwork of tattooed flesh and dermal plating goosebumped in cross-hatch brail. Golden orb in his right eye socket, shutter and nerve connectors of the ocular completely exposed. Jagged pink scar tissue outlined every implant.

"I love everything in this world," the corpse thrower said, "but I was born with organs fragile as wet leaves. My heart, my skin–it's all crumbling. In the next life, I want to climb trees and build a castle of deer hide and circuit boards and I want to ride a dirt bike over rolling hills and fire guns as big as that wild cannon you're holding and I want to feel pain without falling to pieces. So when I die, I'm taking everything with me."

The boy adjusted his grip on the god killer from ready to blast to just dangling at his side. He said, "You do your own mods?"

The corpse thrower said, "Got no choice. See anyone else out here?" He waved his arms around the woods, the clearing of chopped timber where an old world dirt bike leaned against a tin shed with hooks hanging from the ceiling, rancid black-red mud below. A teepee decorated in the guts of old world tech: scratched and sun-warped CDs, busted keyboards, circuitry that sparkled in the sunlight.

The boy said, "Could you take a look at my dad?"

The corpse thrower led the boy and his sleeping father into his tent. Said, "Drop him there. On the table, not the cot."

The boy dropped the man on top of a weather-worn and deeply scarred wooden table, then he dropped all their shit in a pile on the dirt floor and swung his arm around in several rotations to loosen it up and he breathed a sigh of relief. The teepee was stitched-together deer hides stretched over a wooden frame. Runes and sigils drawn in blood and oil all over the walls. Mushrooms sprouted from cave painting patterns of mold in the beams.

The corpse thrower rummaged through a heap of chrome and rusted steel junk. An arm in worse shape than the boy's, a couple legs with stiff hydraulics and loose screws, cables and plastic shell casings of various sizes. The corpse thrower dug out four hubcaps, each with three wire-tangled spikes poking out of the bowl sides. He stacked them on the ground next to the table and grabbed a sawzall from a cluttered toolbox. Squeezed the trigger to test the battery. The thing went yin-yin-yin-yin as a rusty blade rapidly oscillated.

The corpse thrower said, "You hungry? There's stew in the pot outside."

The boy said, "What exactly are you going to do with him?"

"I scanned the both of you soon as you walked up on me. Your dad's never going to move his arms and legs again. Most of his nerves are shot. Muscles are baked. Best

I can do for you is lighten the load so you can carry him back to the city. Find a doc to hook him up with some decent chrome." The corpse thrower held up one of the hubcaps, said, "These will work as protective nubs to keep infection out. The little tendrils will wire into his nervous system, keep a charge going so his brain doesn't think he's dead."

The boy pulled the revolver from his waistband and upped it in the corpse thrower's face.

The corpse thrower said, "What's this for?"

The boy nodded to the scrap pile. Said, "You've got limbs over there that'll work just fine. When me and my dad walk out of here, we're both walking out."

The corpse thrower said, "I don't fucking think so. I'm way out here on my own, and with my condition. When I lose function in my arms and legs–and it is a matter of when–I'll need a back-up."

The boy's hand shook, his face twisted in rage. "Fuck," he said. "What about that gun over there? The big one. I'll trade you for the legs alone. Keep the arms."

"I've got no use for a weapon of that caliber. When I take a shot at something, I prefer the body to still be there. But I will give you this." The corpse thrower pulled a small pancake-shaped device from his pocket and pressed a button. The chest at the foot of his cot lifted off the ground and floated over to hover behind his knees. The corpse thrower said, "It's a tractor fob. The chest follows its signal. Make it easier on yourself, since you'll still be lugging the old man around."

The boy took the tractor fob. Tucked the revolver. Sniffed. "I'm sorry," he said.

"Don't ever say sorry, kid. I'm only giving it to you 'cause I can tell you mean to use that thing, even after what I told you about the bombs."

The boy nodded. "I'm going to eat some stew."

The corpse thrower said, "You go do that."

The boy kissed his father on the forehead and exited the tent and the hover chest followed him.

The corpse thrower ran another scan on the man. Touched his chest. "Hold on," he said to himself, "What's this now?"

The man's eyes shot open and trembled in panic. He rolled his head to one side and then the other, said, "Where the fuck am I?"

The corpse thrower clapped a hand over the man's mouth and said, "Shh, sh, sh. Your boy brought you here. Your limbs don't work and I'm going to have to saw them off, but you'll live. You'll feel the sensation of phantom limbs and frequent spasms, but you'll live."

The man bit the corpse thrower's hand and when he yanked it away, the man hollered for the boy, and the boy came running with a mouthful of deer stew.

The corpse thrower said, "See? I'm even feeding him. There's plenty for both of you, asshole."

The man said, "Son."

The boy tried to think of something to tell the man, but he couldn't think of anything because he was the son and this was his dad and it was supposed to be the other way around, the man telling the boy it'd be okay, it'll all be over soon and we'll be on our way, and one day things will be much better than they are now, but we'll stick it out together, we'll make it.

The boy swallowed the stew and said, "I'm sorry, dad." He stood near the man's head and stroked his hair and cried. "I don't know what else to do."

The man was quiet for a while. He couldn't move his arms to wrap them around the boy and console him and he thought, The fuck do I need them for if I can't do that?

"Go eat," he said. "It'll be okay. You did good, bringing us here."

The boy kissed his father's temple and wiped his face on his sleeve and left.

The corpse thrower said, "How much can you feel?"

The man said, "What's that matter? You got some knockout mist, a bootleg Head Trip?"

The corpse thrower said, "That shit'll rot your brain. And no, I have neither. Can you feel this?" He pressed the tip of the blade into the man's left bicep.

The man said, "Sort of."

The corpse thrower said, "Then I apologize. I'll keep talking to you so you don't pass out. What would you like me to talk about?"

"You ever love anyone?" the man said.

"I did once, yeah," the corpse thrower said.

"Tell me about her."

"So you enjoy pain," the corpse thrower said, squeezing the trigger of the saw and gripping the man's left arm. He held the arm straight out and began cutting through it-blood spattering all over his face and pooling on the dirt floor-and he said over the man's screams and the whirring of the saw, "So this fucking bitch..."

Outside, the boy sat near the cooking fire, hands cupped over his ears, and he chewed on tough chunks of deer meat and rocked himself back and forth.

XXIII

W ITH HIS FATHER STRAPPED to his back and facing the opposite direction, the boy feared what his silence could mean, so he tried to keep him talking. He said, "Tell me another story about mom."

And the man gave sort of a weak chuckle, said, "I thought it would be romantic for us to ride out to the crash site. The crater out in the desert where the piece of the moon had landed. But I wasn't too good a judge at how far outside the city it was. You could see the lip of the crater from so many places in the city. It didn't seem that far away. But we set out—and I was tryna surprise her the whole time, told her hop on the bike and didn't say where we were going—and we were miles away from the crater still when the bike ran out of fuel. Your mom was so pissed at me. We'd gone too far to turn back without even taking a look at what I'd dragged her out there for. And so we walked the rest of the way. Probably three miles of rocky desert. And when we finally made it to the crater, we had to climb the lip of it, which was skyscraper high and shot damn near straight up and we kept slipping and your mom snapped at me about how her feet were bleeding and I felt like such an ass, but we'd already come so far, you know. If we could just get up over the lip. If my bike hadn't run out of gas, we could have driven up the side of it. But it just wasn't happening. It was too steep and too smooth to climb. I told your mom how sorry I was and we slid down on our backs to the base of the crater and your mom pointed up to the sky. Neither of us had seen a star before, but that far outside the city in the pitch black desert, the sky was full of them. She seemed so serene. Eventually, we walked back to the bike and pushed it back to the city, whole time looking up at the stars, not even thinking bout our bleeding feet or the crater we couldn't climb."

XXIV

THE BOY GREW DIZZY under the weight of his father. Kept his head down. Tried to block out everything but his steps and his breathing. Heard a branch snap to his left and looked up and froze. The man twisted and craned his neck and the boy held up an iron finger to shush him. Slowly turned sideways so the man too could see the two-headed buck. Forty-point rack between the twin heads. Same creature they'd crossed and let go before, now here it was again, close enough to reach out and touch. They all stood staring a few beats, breathless. An ear on each of the heads twitched. And then the creature bent at the knees and sprang to the side, sprinting in a zig-zag pattern and dipping off into the safety of the thick brush. The boy reached up to squeeze his father's shoulder and the man snorted a chuckle, his eyes going red and glassy.

XXV

F ALLEN CABLES AT THE base of a black tree. Roots clawing up from the dirt. Ruts dug out by wild mutant boars and rocks over slick mud. Damn near everything along the forest floor threatened to snap an ankle at any given misstep, so the boy kept his head on a swivel between his feet and their surroundings. They trekked rolling hills of crispy blond grass and spotted a rollercoaster encroaching on the wooded landscape, spiraling into the sky behind a tall chain-link fence entwined in yellow weeds.

The man said, "Let's cut through," and so they cut through the amusement park, past the faded cartoon animal cut-outs and the bumper cars covered in green moss and the try-your-luck ring toss booth lined with plastic bags of fish skeletons and they stood beneath the rollercoaster and gazed up at how it looped and coiled against the colorless sky.

The man said, "Go flip that switch," and the boy said, "Dad," and the man said, "Come on, just try it."

The boy struggled with the switch. Took the hydraulics in his left hand to flip it up in a rusted screech. Nothing happened.

The man said, "Check the breaker box."

The boy said, "Dad-" and he wanted to tell him how stupid this was, but he knew what the man was trying to do, because they'd been here before, and it had been simple as a breaker needing to be replaced in the dusty maintenance closet, and the

three of them had ridden the slow crawl
to the top-the boy held tightly in the arms
of his mother, too small to be held in by
the bars-and he could barely remember
that far back but he could remember the
feeling like being carried through the air
by some benevolent beast, his little self
flung in spinning death circles as the
world blurred past. He could remember the
laughter underneath her screams.

The boy said, "I'm good with
remembering, dad. We don't have to-"

And then the train of carts stuttered
forward and there was the rattling
and clanking of ancient machinery they
shouldn't be climbing into, probably, but
the thing was picking up speed already and
the boy just wanted to get this over with,
or he wanted to go back to that memory
to feel the ghost of her wrapped around
him, keeping him safe, and so he clicked
the tractor fob to drop the hover crate on

the ground and he unclipped his dad from his back–the limbless man saying, "Just drop me down here so I can watch," and the boy saying, "Fuck that, you're coming with"–and the boy leapt into the cart at the tail end and dropped the man in the seat next to him just as the train made its first ascension at an eighty-degree angle, lurching the boy backwards and nearly tossing the man out the bottom, saved by the boy's grip around his shoulders.

They laughed nervously together and then the boy howled as they reached the peak, the train rocking back and forth in an anxiety-inducing stall just before the drop.

All the noise brought out the moon drinkers. They spilled from the shadows of the fun house and those hiding in the woods clamored over the fence. They ran at full sprint, some falling over each other. At least a dozen of them, all milky white eyes and gnashing teeth. Webs of blue veins over translucent faces. Crazed mutants who'd drank of the lunar water back when it was believed you could boil the poison out of it, which had worked okay for some, sure. But for the unlucky, a sick stomach turned to fever dreams of ripping the flesh off your family members and then eventually dreams of nothing but static, a head full of parasites in control of a spastic body that only wanted to block out the light and noise of the world, to eat in the dark–perpetually hungry and sleepless. These unlucky ones had never seen the mercy of a smoking gun in their lover's hand. Never heard the crying protests of their son who'd grow to believe the lies he told himself of what happened to his mom. Or of what his dad did.

The man and the boy saw them as a crawling wave of cockroaches in an image that spun upside down then right side up in three neck-snapping rotations.

The moon drinkers climbed up the legs of the rollercoaster, propelling themselves over one another until a couple stood on the tracks, in the way of the train coming round again. One of the moon drinkers, a woman with thin hair and a tattered dress, went under the front cart, the wheels chomping one of her legs to bits until the old machinery couldn't swallow anymore bone and the whole thing grinded to a halt in front of a small child.

The boy strapped his father to his back and leapt off the ride onto the platform. The child who had at first seemed dazed now pounced across the carts, biting at the air like a rabid animal, the deflated red balloon wrapped around his wrist flapping behind him.

The boy hit the tractor fob and the crate full of guns hovered above the ground and followed behind them as the boy sprinted for the park entrance, ducking and weaving between outstretched arms of moon drinkers.

He hopped a bench and kicked a fat fucker in the face, knocking him back on top of another moon drinker.

Strapped to the boy's back, the man watched the stampede closing in on them. "You're not outrunning this, son," he said. "You'll have to fight."

The boy swooped the lid off a trash can with his iron hand and spun, flicking it like a frisbee into the herd. The lid bounced between a couple heads before breaking the teeth in a clown's mouth. The child with the balloon pounced on top of the hover crate speeding behind them. Out of reflex, the man tried kicking him off and remembered he had no legs. They were past the entrance now and booking it for the woods, weaving between trees and breaking off in one direction then another, choosing the paths of harsher terrain and obstacles to widen the gap between themselves and the moon drinkers. Whole time, the child with the balloon clung to the hover crate, swiping at the man's face.

"Kid," the man said.

"What?" the boy said.

"Kill this kid," the man said.

The boy shot a glance back at what was happening and spun to clothesline the child off of the hover crate. The child sprang to his feet again like it was nothing and pounced on the boy, who grabbed him by the throat with both hands and struggled to keep his gnashing teeth from biting down on his neck, a struggle that went on longer than it needed to before the man said, "He's not there, son. Whoever he was before is gone."

They spun in circles, the child's face up against the boy's face, screaming in agonizing hunger as the woods blurred around them. The boy threw the child to the ground and he sprang back up and the boy kicked the child onto his ass and again the child bounced back and this time the boy swung an iron fist that caved the child's face in at the nose and the child fell on his back, swallowing the teeth knocked loose from his gums, and he didn't get back up again.

The boy doubled over and retched.

The man on his back stared up at the filthy grey sky and didn't ask if, at least for a moment back there, the boy was having fun.

XXVI

THE MAN NODDED IN and out. Back of his head butting against the boy's. The boy hit the torch, unconcerned whether or not his father noticed. The pain-erasing euphoria trailing the spike of adrenaline and endorphins was exactly the shit he needed to keep going. So he hit the torch, blowing smoke signals up to nobody, until he felt that burning splash at the back of his throat that told him the kaza was cashed.

They came to a stream much wider than the creek of bodies they'd crossed before. Rocks too slippery/slanted/sporadic to cross the torrent crashing over them, spattering crystal lunar poison droplets.

The man was stuck watching the path they'd already trampled, but he could hear the water, and what was left of the man's body deflated. He craned his neck, squinted against the sun burst flaring between a teepee of boulders atop an embankment of rocks that grew into a mountain. "We'll have to climb," he said.

The boy spat. His shoulders ached and his chest rattled and he could feel his lungs scraping against his ribcage and his legs shook and his lips were chapped, bloody tally marks of dead skin. But the kaza in his system said fuck all that. Eyes wide and heart racing, every nerve popping off with high-voltage electricity.

"It's only if you drink it," the boy said, and he stepped into the stream, the chill of it biting everywhere below his abdomen as his feet were sucked straight to the bottom.

He focused all his strength in the ball of his left foot and in lifting his right leg to kick slow motion through the current, like wading through concrete, and he took one step at a time just like that while the violent flow rocked him side to side, the man thrashing and yelping on his back.

"What are you doing?!" the man screamed.

And the boy barked back, "Who is carrying who?!"

Waves like hammers against his ribs until at least one of them cracked. The boy planted both feet and lurched forward with a roar through the last bit of shallow stream and once they were back on dry land, he buckled at the knees and punched pockets into the mud and he wheezed until he caught his breath.

The man watched the raging torrent with nothing more to say.

Poison-drenched clothes clinging to his battered body, the boy grunted to his feet. Adjusted the shoulder straps that held his father. On trembling legs, he pressed on.

XXVII

"SOON AS THE SECOND well is dug," the boy said, "I'm leaving for the city. Me and the girl. There's nothing for us in the village. You should come too. Stay with us, or wherever you stay when you're gone a long time. I know you don't even fuck with the church. Whatever you believed in before died with mom. So just come to the city with us. We'll get jobs. I'm sure they need diggers in the city. Or whatever, we'll find something. We gotta get out, though, right?"

The man said, "We were never believers, me and your mom, even back when we joined the church. It's just that, when we found out we'd be having you—we'd fall asleep to the sounds of shootings and the howls of junkies fried off chems or some glitched-out Head Trip—and we knew we couldn't raise a child in the city. Not the part we could afford to live in. And I was having no luck with the shit I was doing to get us to a better place, if there was such a thing. So we spoke to my sister, your aunt. She was always the nomadic type, was always running off with a lover or a group to live with in the desert or the woods somewhere, but always finding herself dropped back in the slums. Until she met a disciple of the church. When the village was smaller, they'd send younger members down into the city to spread the word and recruit new members. Your aunt was sold on the community shit. Your mom and me, we saw it as our way out. At least it'd be safer, we thought. We were promised jobs and shelter. And the church, they pulled through on everything. But there were issues with the pregnancy. Having a baby wasn't anything we'd planned on, but once it was happening, we were so excited. Then one day we're lying in bed in our new trailer out in the hills, away from all the gunshots and howling junkies, and your mom starts bleeding. And it just keeps flowing, soaking the sheets, the carpet, it's everywhere and then there's these black clumps of tissue sort of like coffee grounds and… your mom lost it. So did I. I did everything I knew to do to get the stains out, but they didn't come all the way out. Your mom wouldn't even sleep in the bed. The church talked big about this keeper of the woods who granted miracles and life and shit, so I ran out into the woods one night. Cut myself at the abdomen and bled into the dirt. Screamed for a god to meet me, let me trade myself. And the god appeared to me. Showed up the same as the sculptures depict, draped in black robes with the skull of a deer. It simply said to return home. And so I ran and your mom met me at the door and she was crying, she said 'feel,' and she grabbed my hand and made me touch her belly, and I felt you move."

XXVIII

THE WOODS ALL LOOKED the same. Every tree was a tangled tower of cables. The brush grew thicker. The hover crate got caught up several times and the boy's jacket was tearing from getting snagged on thorn bushes.

They were lost.

Sitting on a rock with her heels pressed to her butt cheeks, arms wrapped around knees pressed against her tits, the woman in the wolf headdress said, "You're lost, boy."

The boy said, "No shit."

The wolf woman pointed to where the ground sloped higher and plateaued with a crown of trees splitting sun rays. She said, "Climb over and down the other side of that hill and you will enter a valley at the base of a mountain. Walk with your back to the mountain and eventually you'll make it home. You don't have much longer, though. The keeper of the woods will wake after two moons to find an empty altar, unless you can go through with what your father brought you out here for."

The boy said nothing.

The wolf woman bit her lip. Teeth sharpened to points. "Don't you want to know?"

"Know what?" the boy said. "That my dad brought us out here to be eaten by a god?"

The wolf woman raised an eyebrow. "Didn't tag you as a believer."

"The church isn't quiet about it. Or, it is, but the villagers aren't. Everybody knows somebody who's been elected as an offering." The boy adjusted a harness strap and the man's head rolled from his left shoulder to his right. "I just wanted to go hunting with my dad."

"Which way will you play it?" she said.

The boy climbed up and over the hill and entered the valley just as the wolf woman described. Perfect circle of ash and fallen timber at least a dozen acres in diameter and off in the distance was the mountain, casting shade over hills of scrap metal and forested ghost towns. The boy considered which direction he'd head in and then he stuck to the path one step at a time.

XXIX

WHAT THE MAN WANTED to say was, how come he knew the way to the sacrificial mountaintop by heart, was he'd stolen the coordinates after his sister was elected. Made the journey by himself, forgetting to bring any food. He was starved and delirious and high off the altitude by the time he climbed to the offering stone still slick with her blood, and the blood of an elder woman whose mind had been steadily slipping. A symbol of mercy. That's how they liked to pitch it. Except the man's sister was happy. Childless and unwed, but she put in work between the bullet farm and the garden and she drew pictures with charcoal of the nameless mutant beasts in the woods and of the boy as he grew and played. What the man wanted to say was he missed his sister. And much as he had to be grateful for, he had to wonder what kind of god could grant a miracle such as the boy, then demand to be fed the lives of its worshipers. It made sense to the man at one point. He wanted to say that. It all made sense in the way a ritual does when it's working for you. Then he lost his sister, and his lover after that, and what the man wanted to say, is he'd often dreamt of following the next elected to the altar and seeing what a bullet between the eyes of a god would do. What the man wanted to say was that he'd felt lost in the city with all of its advancements innovating new methods of detachment from one's own body and spirit, but that he felt just the same off the grid with the believers. Nature was shit. Jobs and chems and other lost people with their heads full of some uploaded distraction or belief in a god that would eat them alive—all of it was shit. What the man wanted to say was he'd seen and inflicted so much atrocity borne of a nihilistic myopia, excused by his conscience for the need to survive in a cruel world, and the only people who made him see differently were taken from him. He wanted to tell the boy he didn't leave him all the time because he didn't think of him, but that he couldn't stand to look at him every day and see his mother's face. He wanted to ask the boy what he thought about a deity whose greatest blessing to humanity was its own self-perpetuating existence-a bargain of continued allowance to remain in the struggle, of simply not being slaughtered—and in exchange, you had to gamble with that very blessing, with your own life—and when time came that it was your life and the life of the last thing you loved in the whole filthy fucking world that was to be paid in blood—the man wanted to ask the boy if such a gamble was even worth it. But the man could barely speak. The thing in his chest beat intermittently. He closed his eyes. Took all the strength he had in him, but what he finally said to the boy before he nodded off was, "She'd be so proud of you."

XXX

THEY CAME UPON ANOTHER ghost town. Least a dozen blocks of row homes, several missing a roof or casting their shadows over fallen bricks. Asphalt streets cracked in a broken plate pattern. Potholes full of lunar poison water. There was a playground with rusty swing sets and sun-bleached slides and skeletal trees stood here and there but they were unplugged and hollow, could be toppled into a pile of soft splinters with the slightest shove. In the center of town stood a church with dust-caked stained-glass windows and a fountain full of garbage.

The boy clasped his iron hand over his nose and mouth, breathing in that dirty penny smell to mask the rancid dumpster-bottom miasma that hung in the air, so thick you could see it in waves. The boy asked which way they should go. This felt very much in the wrong direction. But the man did not answer. The boy stood still for a long time to be sure he felt his father's breathing against his back. The man was in a deep sleep with the sun beating down on his face. The boy clicked off the tractor fob in his pocket and the cargo chest hovering behind them dropped to the ground and he turned and knelt down to open it, grunting under his father's weight. He took out the holomap and pressed a button but the screen remained dark. He closed the chest and set the tablet face-up on the lid so the sun could juice it back up. Then he took the pistol from his waistband, iron hand back over his mouth, and walked to the nearest row home. Used the pistol to part the bindweed curtain over the door and stepped inside. He searched cabinets and dresser drawers more out of curiosity than any hope of finding something valuable. Corroded batteries, dead cockroaches, paper money. All junk. In one of the rooms was a mattress and nothing else. Dark brown stain the size of a body. The boy flipped the mattress over. Springs twisting up through thin fabric. He went outside and unclasped his father from his back and set him down in the shade of a bus stop awning and sat on the bench beside him.

XXXI

I T WAS ALMOST SUNDOWN before the holomap's light shone green and the boy fired it up while the limbless man continued to snore next to him. Little glowing replicas of the buildings around them grew out of the screen. Arrow hovering over the bus stop pointed in the direction they faced. The boy pinched the center of the map and then spread his fingers open, zooming out. A star hovered above a mountainous region only a few miles outside the ghost town and when the boy pressed the star, an image flashed on screen of stone slabs stacked at the edge of a cliff and he knew it was the altar the wolf woman had spoken of. He zoomed out again to be sure the arrow pointed towards the star and then he strapped his father to his back and continued walking. Night fell by the time they entered the woods again. The boy stopped to build a fire.

XXXII

THE MAN WOKE WITH a thirst-rattled gasp that startled the boy, who sat stirring the fire with an iron finger. Propped up by the surface roots of a tree neither of them could name, the man waved his chrome-capped nubs, kicking and clawing his way from a nightmare where he still had arms and legs. He realized where he was and turned his face from the boy, then they both looked up past the shadows of branches clasped like hands to the glow of the broken moon. Dozens of stars dotted the sky, some in clusters as many as five. More than the boy had ever seen at one time.

"What do you think it was like before the moon split?" the boy said. "Not just the sky, I mean, but everything."

"I have a hard time imagining."

"You think things were better back then?"

The man thought on it for a bit. Then he said, "Probably not."

The boy lay in the dirt near his father's lap and watched the fire until he drifted to sleep and in the morning, he snuffed out the last of the embers with the heel of his boot and he strapped his father onto his back and they walked on.

XXXIII

T HE BOY SAID, "TELL me another story about mom."

XXXIV

THEY'D BEEN QUIET FOR a while, both exhausted—the man from all the blood loss and phantom limb spasms, the boy from carrying his father on his back. But then the man screamed.

"Oh, god!" he said, clouds of smoke seeping through his shirt. "This hurts so much worse than I thought it would!"

A trill of electric popping noises, then his chest erupted in a bloody gush of fragmented bone and glistening shards of chrome. The man's thrashing sent the boy to his hands and knees and he froze there as pieces of his father's mechanical heart rained down around him. Stench of overcooked meat and melted plastic.

The man was quiet again.

The boy unbuckled the harness and his father's limbless torso slid off his back and fell face down in the dirt.

It was a long time before the boy rolled him over. A long time after that before he caught his breath and wept with his father's blood on his lips. Tears falling into the cavity in his father's chest.

XXXV

THE BOY STACKED UP a bed of rocks and lay the mess of what remained of his father on top of it. He built a tent of sticks over the man and doused the pyre with the oil he used for his mechanical joints. He dissected the steel casing of the lung torch and pressed the button to heat the coils and touched the hissing electric glow to his father's kneecaps.

He stepped back and watched the flames consume the man.

The wolf woman said, "You shouldn't have done that."

She appeared like a specter out of the dark, fading in from the treeline.

The boy said, "You're not even real."

The wolf woman wrapped her arms around the boy from behind. Dug her nails in his scalp. Bit his ear. "What makes you think that?" she said.

The boy felt himself getting hard and turned his eyes from the fire. "It's gotta be the kaza fucking with me," he said. "Your existence makes no sense."

"Neither does yours."

She gripped his crotch. Brushed her tits against his back. The hairs on the back of the boy's neck stood up.

The wolf woman sauntered over to the cargo crate and bent to open it. She took out the candy-painted green cell blaster and held it against her hip. "You know what this is?" she said.

"A ghost gun," the boy said. "Can't be scanned or traced. My dad's bought a few of them, but none that big before."

"This is a god killer," the wolf woman said, stepping closer to the boy while waving around the giant gun. "Whether you run or fight, you'll want to hold on tight to this." She held the gun across her upturned palms and offered it to the boy, who took and held it in the same way. Admired the way its gaudy metallic sheen caught the light of the fire.

"How long before it wakes up?" the boy said.

The wolf woman looked to the half moon and said, "Not long." She pointed to the road past the treeline, a jagged dirt road that stretched out like a tongue from the mouth of a cave and only ran a short stretch. "That's its takeoff," the wolf woman said. "The road is carved into the earth by the finger of god itself, dug fresh again each time it flies from the cave with its claws hung low. The debris littered along the road is ash and bone dust that falls from its body when the god ascends."

The boy looked from the road to the gun in his hands to the wolf woman. Said, "Who are you?"

"There is no word in your tongue for it," she said. "I could say I am a part of the very god you wish to kill, but so are you." She nodded at the fire that'd grown tall as the trees. "And so was he. And that would make us part of each other. You might consider me an idea. Or a curse."

The boy watched the fire a long time, his father's empty stump turned to shadow inside the raging flames. Then he said to the wolf woman, "Will you help me?"

She said, "It's suicide, what you're thinking."

He said, "Yeah. So, will you?"

She said, "I'll do what I can," and she turned and disappeared into the trees.

XXXVI

THE BOY WALKED OUT to the middle of the road padded with crushed bones and ash and he sat lotus position with the god killer draped across his lap. Wind fanning the flames of his father's funeral pyre at his back. He faced the mouth of the cave that swallowed the road and he waited for the starving god to wake up.

XXXVII

HOURS PASSED. THE BOY'S eyelids grew heavy and his stomach rumbled and he had to piss, but he refused to move. Probably couldn't even if he wanted to—legs gone numb under the weight of the god killer. His body had never felt more like a temporary shell than now, and so to buckle at its needs seemed ludicrous. A stream of piss trickled from the cuff of his jeans. The road ahead stretched out into pitch black, but daybreak would be coming soon enough.

XXXVIII

SHADOWS DISSIPATED IN THE light of the rising sun and the boy stood and aimed up the road, anticipating the rush of a wailing demon taking flight, or the earth-rattling footfalls of a raging behemoth. Instead, the keeper of the woods appeared as a man. The boy's vision blurred. He wiped his eyes with his sleeve and upped the gun again with shaking hands. The man continued to approach calmly until the long barrel touched his chest and he stopped and said, "Do you want to hear another story about your mom?"

XXXIX

THE BOY DROPPED THE god killer and fell to his knees. Exhausted and alone. A child in need of his parents. The god who resembled his father placed a hand on the boy's head and said, "It'll be okay, son," and the boy's eyes welled with tears.

Hiding behind a tree, the wolf woman slid her fingers inside her pussy and pulled out a jagged sword made of bone, other hand over her mouth to muffle her moaning. When the entire length of the dripping blade was out, she gripped the handle in both hands. Held the sword out in front of her. Crept up on the man from behind. Calloused feet planted in the dirt and ash and bone dust, she raised the bone sword over her head, twisted her hips for the swing aimed at the man's neck.

A pair of wings like black leather sails tore through the man's sweater and spread wide at his sides, deflecting the sword. The left wing bent like an arm at the elbow and the sharp tip of it shot up under the wolf woman's jaw and she spat out blood. The wing retracted and she fell to her knees, mirroring the boy, the pupils of their wide eyes dilating in panic.

The flesh around the man's right hand crumbled and fell from a skeletal grey paw with long, razor-tipped fingers. He knelt between the boy and the wolf woman. He winked at the boy, then he dug his claws into the wolf woman's chest. Wet crunching noises as he twisted and tore her beating heart from the hole he'd punched between her tits. The man took a bite of the heart as the wolf woman's eyes rolled back and she folded forward, contorted limbs pointing in every direction.

The man swallowed. A sick gurgling rose from the back of his throat. He smiled at the boy with red teeth. Offered the rest of the heart that pulsed in his paw, squirting from severed arteries.

But the boy was in two different places at that moment–there on his knees in the dirt before god, and in another life, riding on his father's back through the woods, his mother plucking a beetle from a tree saying, "Do you know what this is?" and the boy's shrill toddler voice saying, "It's a bug!" and the three of them laughing–and the boy on his knees before god felt around in the dark until his mechanical fingers found the grip of a massive candy-painted green cell blaster that'd been rumored to kill gods, and with a tear falling from his eye, he said to the father the god resembled,

"I'll see you again soon," and he raised the blaster as the god sprang to his feet and then the boy pulled the trigger.

A delay of a couple seconds stretched on forever as the god killer made a high-pitched whirring noise and then a glowing orange cartridge the size of a soup can was fired from the wide hexagonal barrel. The kick of it sent the boy rolling backwards for several feet. The round tore through the god's folded wings and got stuck in a tree.

Another delay, then an explosion.
Confetti of splinters.
The blast and flying debris ripped one side of the man's face off, revealing the deer skull beneath.

Growling, the god charged the boy. Scooped him up in his arms and hovered just above the ground as he shot forward, scalping the back of the boy's head against the rocks and the packed dirt and then flinging him against a boulder to the tune of every bone in his back cracking.

The boy gasped for air, iron grasp still clinging tightly to the god killer. Oil bled from a severed hose in his elbow as the cylinders in his arm pumped and clanked in a struggling effort to raise the gun.

The god marching towards him morphed back into his father, wings retracted and flesh repaired, and he gripped the boy's throat in both hands and squeezed. The boy cursed the god in raspy gurgles and smacked his organic fist against the man's side.

The man chuckled. "That is just pathetic, son," he said. "You aren't even worthy of being an offering."

The boy couldn't raise his iron arm, but he could still use his fingers, could still pull the trigger. A whirring charge, and then the blast sent them both rolling sideways, the man's grasp slipping from the boy's throat.

They staggered to their feet and approached each other. Gun dragging behind the boy, stuck in his iron clutch. His shoulder plate slipping, barely hanging on by a few wires. Back of his head ripped clean down to the skull, a streak of red down the back of his shirt.

The man said, "You're making this worse on yourself."

With his organic hand, the boy pulled the revolver from his waistband-black and yellow, mom's little b-and fired all six rounds into the man's face. A hole in the left cheek. Right eye, cratered. Red roses full of meat and bone blooming out the back of his head.

When the man stood toe-to-toe with the boy, he looked at him through the gaping cavity of a dripping, obliterated skull. The boy tossed the empty revolver and punched inside the cavity of the man's head and gripped his larynx from the inside. Squeezed as hard as he could.

Again, the god sprouted its wings and spread them wide. A hole torn through the center of each. A deer skull grew from the cavity of the man's face and swallowed the boy's arm. Hollow eyes staring at him as they flew straight up, the rest of the man's body slipping from the god's beast-like form and falling to the forest floor like molted snakeskin. On their ascent through the tops of the trees, the boy swung his iron arm to brush against a humming cable draped across the branches like a vine. A jolt of intense electricity/the shadow of his skull flashing blue under his skin/the current rushing through his arm into the god's mouth. The god spat the boy across the cloudless, colorless sky and the boy rolled in the air until the barrel of the god killer rested between his knees and he aimed for the head of the god darting towards him and squeezed the trigger.

The whirring of the charge.

The orange glow emitting from the barrel.

The mouth of god spreading wide.

The blast launched the boy further across the sky as the god swallowed the hot glowing round. Skull crumbled to bits as a great ball of light swelled from the god's neck, rippling out an explosion that toppled trees and sent the boy flying ever further, high above the rushing torrent of the god's blood that flooded the woods, washing over the trailers and trading posts in the village, filling the holes dug in search of water all over the hill country, then spilling down from the hills into the streets of the city, where beneath a red traffic light a man looked up into the sky to see a meteor of meat hurling straight towards him and he said oh shit oh no oh fuck not again as a boy wielding a massive gun rumored to kill gods crashed through his windshield and the red river flowed with enough force to pancake cars on impact, to crush the bones and chrome of the punks and the hobos and the women clutching their babies at the bottom of the flood, skyscrapers soon swallowed by the rising tide, a city of neon glowing dimly beneath a film of crimson, the boy's broken body somewhere along the bottom being filled with the blood, his lungs and stomach taking it in as the voices of his mother and father called out to him from somewhere high above, from the place he severed his own heavy arm and abandoned the god killer for a chance to reach, kicking and thrashing in the blood, swimming higher and higher, following the bubbles of his own silent screams until his head broke the red river's surface, now still and glistening beneath a radiant sun, all the blood the boy had swallowed erupting from the pit of his stomach. He floated on his back, basking in the warmth of the sun and the red river that carried him, and when he finally caught his breath, the god opened his eyes.

MERCY

AFTERWORD
The Making of MERCY

AUTUMN FOLIAGE IN NORTH Texas is all crispy blond and brown. Just dry. I scoped the hills through a thirty-aught-six. Caught view of some kind of bird—a blue one, I don't really know birds—and I pulled my phone out and snapped a pic through the scope. My brother laughed at me, but only with his shoulders and face. Trying not to make too much noise.

There's a lot of lulls in the rhythm of a hunt. We got restless and did some walking.

Taking turns who had their head on a swivel, who was watching our steps.

We came up on a clearing same time as this eight-point buck, almost close enough to reach out and touch. My brother's hand flew to my chest and we stood frozen, breathless. Less than a dozen steps between the two of us and this king of the forest, who stood still as we were. All of us staring.

My brother slowly raised his rifle. Focused down the sights. The earth quit spinning and everything fell silent. Then my brother's shoulders went slack and he lowered the rifle. The buck's ears twitched before he dipped back into the safety of the brush.

I didn't ask what happened, why didn't he take the shot, because I already knew.

But then he said it anyway. "I have never been that close before."

We'd cross paths with the same buck later on that day, and this time there'd be no pause as he stretched his neck towards something he'd barely get a taste of hanging from a tree. Can't remember what he could have been going for; the trees were all skeletal and naked. But before bagging and tagging the king, there was another long lull, of my brother and I talking shit between long drags of silence.

The idea for *Mercy* first hit me during one of these quiet moments. I told my brother about this story idea for a human sacrifice disguised as a hunting trip, an Abraham and Isaac story where a suicidal widower is tasked by a hillbilly cult leader with delivering himself and his son to a sacrificial altar in the woods to keep some ancient, bloodthirsty god satiated.

My brother said, "Damn, you should write that," so I decided yeah, I would.

Other shit came between—*Letting Out the Devils* and some fucking around on collaborative projects—but *Mercy* was steady percolating. Discussing it with the Broken River crew gave it more layers.

J. David Osborne said the next wave is cyberpunk. So *Mercy* became cyberpunk.

E Rathke built a world in which the moon split in half and fell to earth and a black tree forest full of mutated creatures grew out of the wreckage. He put this lore in the Broken River shared folder of manuscripts and ideas and so there was another sandbox *Mercy* would play in.

David Simmons been steady genre-hopping with banger after banger that retains his unique voice despite the setting or premise, so I thought *bet, I can do that. It's time to write a post-apocalyptic / cyberpunk / hillbilly cult horror novel.*

Grant Wamack and I been digging out of similar trenches lately, getting it out the mud by any means, grinding tirelessly sunup to sundown. *Mercy* had to reflect this, had to work as a ritual of turning the tables of fortune. (Grant's writing has also influenced the sexual content of my work recently, which I don't know how to say without it sounding weird, but it's like a competitive thing to include at least one pornographically steamy scene... I regret admitting this. Moving on).

December 1 became the deadline to drop JDO's *Dying World* and *Mercy* at the same time. This was in October maybe. I put the book up for pre-order and got serious on it. In the meantime, there was *Cyberpunk 2077* and a four-years-running *Fallout 4* play-through that sort of represented and influenced the look of this world in my head. Meantime, in comes E Rathke being like, "I'll write a cyberpunk thing by then, too," which is the true origin story of *Howl*, a banger that exists as evidence to homie's ability to spit out a book off the top of the dome in a very short amount of time. I mean, yeah, I had just begun writing *Mercy* for real, but the ideas and notes had existed for a year.

But anyway. The book gets written, mostly. I've got the premise. I've got what I think is the right ending to pull off the table-turning ritual. I've got December 1 rushing up quick because, lowkey, my wife Erika and I found out this year we'd be having our second son—a happy accident—and all of a sudden, the book that's about to drop stops hitting for me. I don't really fuck with it so much. I type to get the word count up, flesh out my ideas, but it's not right. And mostly I'm backspacing, staring at that cursor going blink blink blink at the end of a paragraph I don't care to show the world.

So I trash it.

Delete the whole thing. No new file, no copy and paste this over to another draft to try and work in another direction, none of that. Five days before the book is supposed to drop, I hit delete and start all over.

Because this is a story of going toe to toe with god and upping a giant gun in his face. So that's what I had to do in order to write such a thing: I had to let the odds stack up against me and fight like hell. I didn't sleep for three days, then I slept for two hours and got back at it. I was getting that tweaker high of being up on amphetamines for way too long, a state I hadn't existed in for going on a decade. I craved sleep and for this book to just be done with, flushed out of my system. And why'd I do this to myself again?

I thought I knew what the story was. A father and son story. A look at what the hillbillies of a cyberpunk world get up to. Maybe it'd go in the direction of survival horror, maybe it'd go full Berserk crazy. But it wanted to be something more somber, more poetic, much as I was running from that. I wanted to write something fun and stupid, I really did, but this kid happened.

In a month or less, my wife and I will be welcoming Phoenix Asher into the world. His existence in this incarnation has already given me grey hairs and motivated my ass to be more ambitious, while whole time humbling my ass to be more grateful.

We weren't planning on another kid, but the lines on the stick were blue all the same.

Excited, nervous, our first thought was "Damn, we need a bigger house. And some more money." So I got to hustling harder, got to remodeling our thousand square foot starter home to be ready for a whole-ass family of four.

Then soon as the surprise of this child was sinking in, we lost it.

I cleaned the blood off the bed and the carpet while floating somewhere above myself. I made deals with beings on the other side, cut my palms open, drew sigils in the dirt. I held Erika while she wept and wondered aloud the things I was trying to hold in.

A few weeks went by of hating whatever god shook us up just to knock us down. Then came the tremors in her belly. Strong enough even I could touch and feel the movement inside her tightening stomach.

The doctors have wiped record of a pregnancy off the chart. It doesn't make sense to anyone, but you can't deny a baby who fought against god to be here. The first checkup back after losing him, that same baby boy was big and strong and wriggling around like a motherfucker on that monitor.

I don't know what to tell you, because I don't know what to tell myself. The kid was here then he wasn't. And then he was again.

"This... this is the same baby." The doctor had no explanation. Could only state what we were all looking at.

Mercy wanted to be more than a fun detour into a new genre. This kid's tale had to be told. A father and son story when I am a father of two sons can't be half-assed.

So I scratched it five days before release. And what flowed out was what it wanted to be the whole time.

A ritual. An exorcism. A fable for my sons, warriors who could go toe to toe with god and not flinch.

*This afterword originally appeared as a guest essay on **Wolf** (radicaledward.substack.com)*

ABOUT THE AUTHOR

KELBY LOSACK is a blue collar mystic hoodrat from Gulf Coast Texas. Husband, father, Broken River novelist, co-host of Agitator. Find him at kelbylosack.com.

ALSO BY KELBY LOSACK

God Is Wearing Black

Letting Out the Devils

Dead Boy (with J. David Osborne)

The Way We Came In

Heathenish